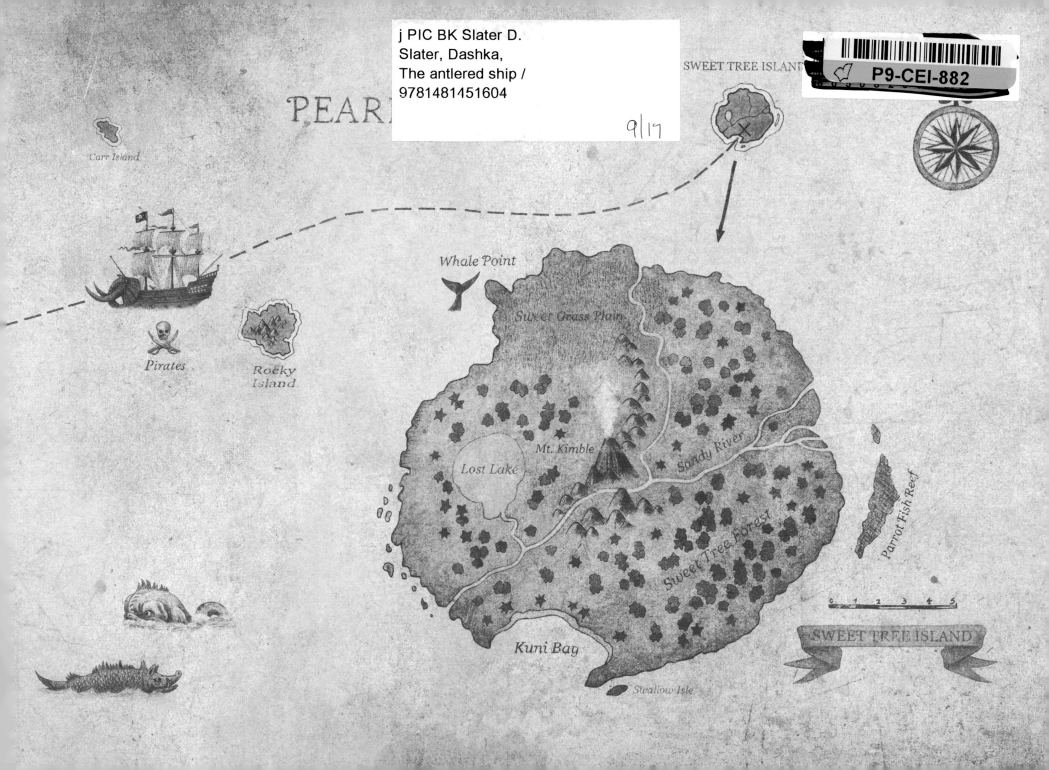

PEARL

SWEET TREE ISLAND

Carr Island

Pirates

Rocky
Island

Whale Point

Sweet Grass Plain

Mt. Kimble

Lost Lake

Sandy River

Sweet Tree Forest

Parrot Fish Reef

Kuni Bay

0 1 2 3 4 5

SWEET TREE ISLAND

Swallow Isle

For my fellow voyagers,
Wendy, Scott, and Stephanie.
With deep gratitude to Andrea, Lauren, Eric, and Terry.
—D. S.

For Kirsten Hall, our North Star.
With special thanks to Andrea, Lauren, and Dashka.
—T. F. & E. F.

BEACH LANE BOOKS • An imprint of Simon & Schuster Children's Publishing Division • 1230 Avenue of the Americas, New York, New York 10020 • Text copyright © 2017 by Dashka Slater • Illustrations copyright © 2017 by Terry Fan and Eric Fan • All rights reserved, including the right of reproduction in whole or in part in any form. • BEACH LANE BOOKS is a trademark of Simon & Schuster, Inc. • For information about special discounts for bulk purchases, please contact Simon & Schuster Special Sales at 1-866-506-1949 or business@simonandschuster.com. • The Simon & Schuster Speakers Bureau can bring authors to your live event. For more information or to book an event, contact the Simon & Schuster Speakers Bureau at 1-866-248-3049 or visit our website at www.simonspeakers.com.
Book design by Lauren Rille
The text for this book was set in Farnham.
The illustrations for this book were rendered in graphite and ballpoint pen, then colored digitally.
Manufactured in China
0617 SCP
First Edition
10 9 8 7 6 5 4 3 2 1
CIP data for this book is available from the Library of Congress.
ISBN 978-1-4814-5160-4 (hardcover)
ISBN 978-1-4814-5161-1 (eBook)

THE ANTLERED SHIP

written by
Dashka Slater

illustrated by
The Fan Brothers

Beach Lane Books • New York   London   Toronto   Sydney   New Delhi

The day the antlered ship arrived,
Marco wondered about the wide world.

He had so many questions.

Why do some songs make you happy and others make you sad?

Why don't trees ever talk?

How deep does the sun go when it sinks into the sea?

But when he posed these questions
to the other foxes, they grew silent.
"What does that have to do with
chicken stew?" they would ask.

So Marco went down to the harbor to see the ship.

Three deer greeted him at the gangplank.

Marco wasn't surprised to learn that they were lost.

"We hope to hire a seaworthy crew," explained Sylvia, the captain.
"I'm afraid we aren't very good sailors."

"I will join you," Marco said. He thought
to himself, *I will search the seas for foxes
who know the answers to my questions.*

A pigeon named Victor volunteered along with his entire flock.
"We want to have adventures," they cooed.

"Welcome aboard," Captain Sylvia said. "We're going to a *wonderful* island,
with tall, sweet grass and short, sweet trees. When we get there, we'll eat
a delectable dinner."

But the voyage was more difficult than anyone expected.

It rained. Waves crashed over the sides of the deck.

Why is water so wet? Marco wondered.

The pigeons weren't used to the hard work
of raising and lowering the sails.
After the first day, they
went belowdecks
to play checkers
and stayed there.

The deer worried about sharp rocks and fierce pirates and feeling seasick. They huddled in the bow and waited for something bad to happen.

After days of drifting
and dining on crackers,
the animals were damp
and cranky.

"We should have stayed in the woods," Sylvia said. "Deer aren't supposed to go to sea."

"We should have stayed in the park," added Victor. "Pigeons aren't supposed to do hard labor."

Marco eyed the deer and the pigeons. "Foxes aren't supposed to be vegetarian," he said. "Still, we must do the best we can."

That evening, Marco found a recipe book in
the galley and cooked a warm and reviving stew.
"Should we look at the charts?" he asked
after everyone had eaten.

CAPTAIN STEFAN

CAPTAIN ANDERS

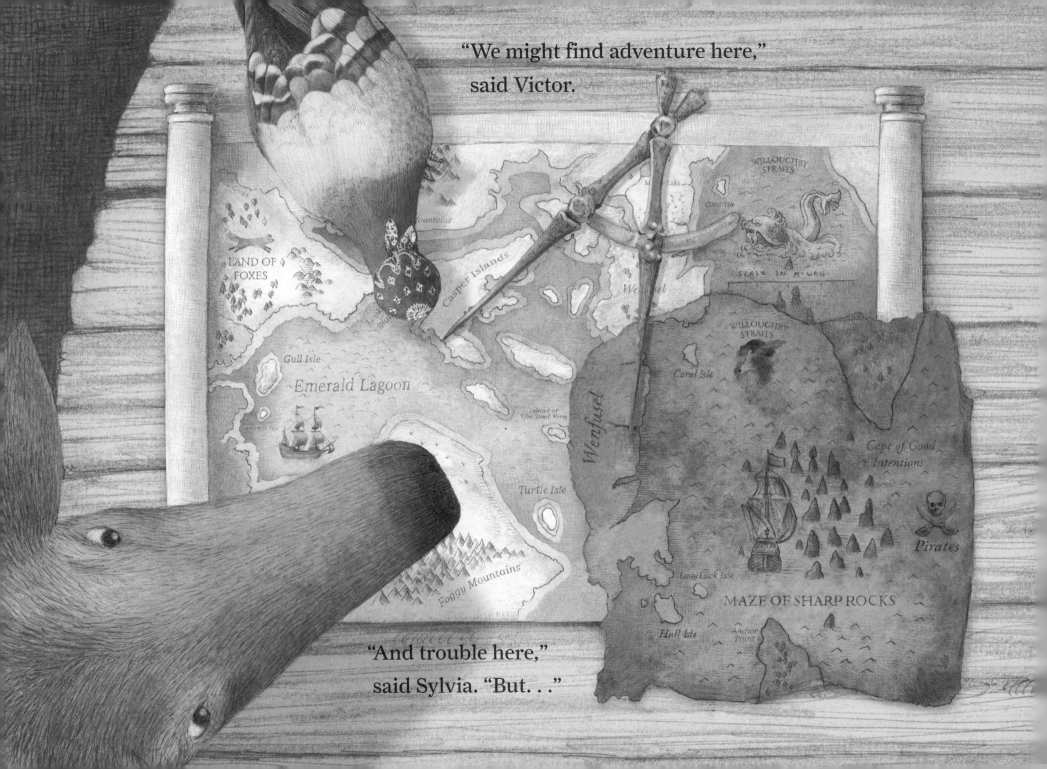

"We might find adventure here,"
said Victor.

"And trouble here,"
said Sylvia. "But. . ."

"we'll find the island with tall, sweet grass and short, sweet trees *here*."

PEARL SEA

Whale Point

Sweet Grass Plain

Lost Lake

Mt. Kimble

Sandy River

Sweet Tree Forest

Parrot Fish Reef

Kuni Bay

0 1 2 3 4 5

SWEET TREE ISLAND

Swallow Isle

And perhaps foxes, too, Marco thought. *Foxes with answers.*

As they plotted their course, the wind picked up.

The storm clouds thinned into marvelous swirls.

"Raise the sails!" Sylvia cried.

In the morning, they came to the Maze of Sharp Rocks,
each one large enough to tear the bottom from the boat.

But the pigeons flew ahead, tracing a path through the shoals and sharp rocks to the safety of the open sea.

The next afternoon, a pirate ship burst from behind a rocky island.

"Turn over yer treasure!" the pirate captain bellowed.

"Or we'll put a hole in yer helm!"

"Lower the antlers!"
Sylvia commanded.

The ships clashed
and crashed and smashed . . .

until the pirates turned and fled.

That evening, an island
appeared on the horizon
with tall waving grasses
and short swaying trees.
"We've found it!" Sylvia cried.
"We've triumphed," Victor cooed.
"Do you see any foxes?"
Marco asked.

The deer grazed the grass and nibbled the trees.
The pigeons told stories of their adventures
to a flock of admiring seagulls.

Marco scoured the island for foxes.

But he didn't find any.

"I have failed,"
Marco told Victor and Sylvia.
"No foxes. No one to answer
 my questions."
"What questions?" Victor asked.

Marco took a deep breath. "Do islands like being alone?

Do waves look more like horses or swans?

And what's the best way to find a friend you can talk to?"

"That last one's easy," Sylvia said.

"You make friends by eating together."

"I disagree," said Victor. "You make friends by having

adventures together."

"Maybe you're both right," Marco said.

"But I think you make friends by asking them questions."

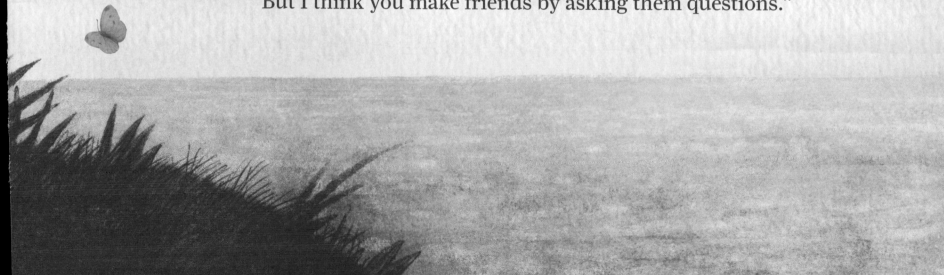

"Well then," mused Sylvia,

"should we head home tomorrow?

Or should we visit the Island of Scrumptious Shrubbery?"

"Are two adventures enough?" asked Victor.

"Or should we have at least one more?"

"Is it better to know what's going to happen?"

wondered Marco. "Or better to be surprised?"

There were so many questions left to answer.
And so many more to ask.

So in the morning,
they raised the anchor
and hoisted the heavy sails.
They knew now that the wind
would come and go,
the clouds would sometimes
make marvelous swirls
and sometimes make them wet,
and that everything they hoped to find
could be found aboard an antlered ship . . .

on the way to wherever they were going.